TILDA
TRIES AGAIN

TOM PERCIVAL

BLOOMSBURY
CHILDREN'S BOOKS

LONDON   OXFORD   NEW YORK   NEW DELHI   SYDNEY

Tilda's world was just
as she liked it.

She had her friends,

her books

and her toys.

Everything was
just right.

Until one day, Tilda's world turned . . .

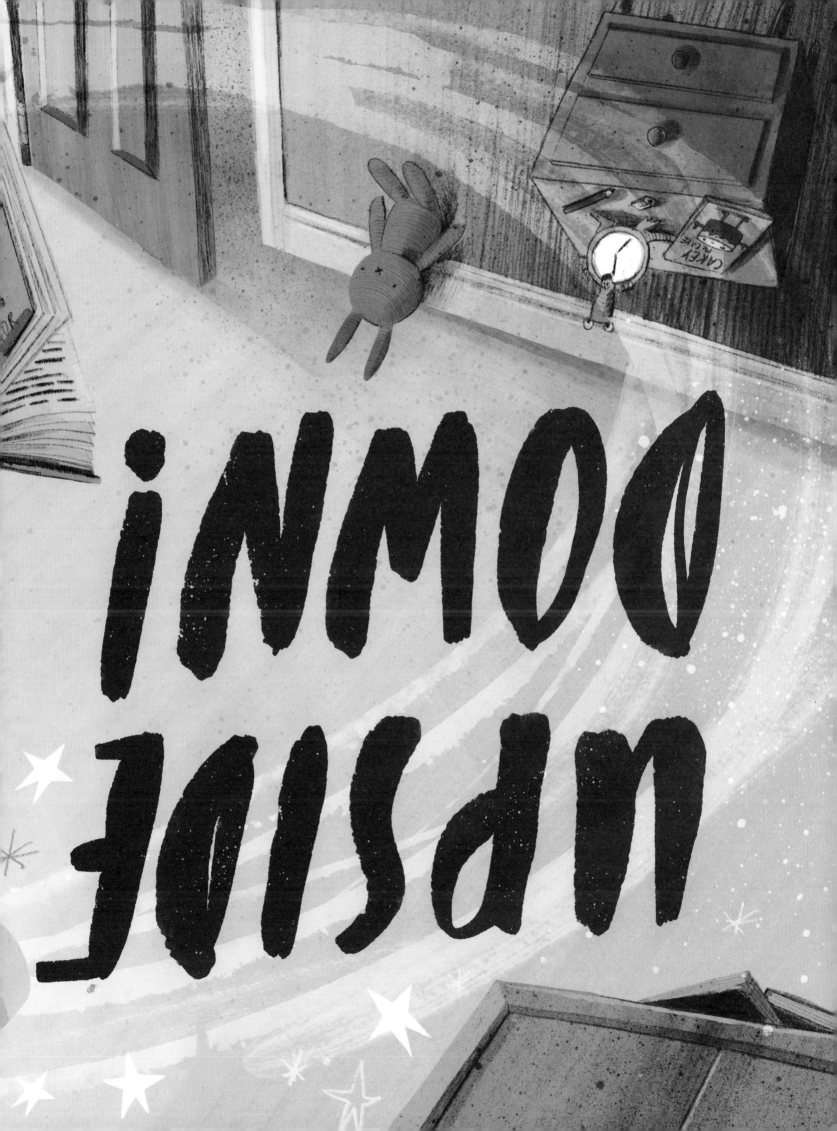

All of a sudden, everything was topsy turvy.

And *nothing* felt right anymore.

Things that had once seemed simple
now felt *incredibly* difficult.

Tilda didn't feel like seeing her friends.

In fact, she didn't feel like
doing anything.

Everything just seemed
TOO hard.

Eventually, Tilda gave up
and decided to do . . .

Then one day, Tilda saw a ladybird
stuck on its back. Its tiny legs
waggled in the air.

"Poor little thing," she said.
"You're all topsy turvy . . .

just like me."

As Tilda tried to work out how to help,
the ladybird wriggled and struggled.

It was no use.
Tilda's heart sank.

But then, the ladybird
tried again.

And again,

and again.

Until at last . . .

It flew free!

Tilda thought about this.
The ladybird hadn't given up . . .

so neither would she!

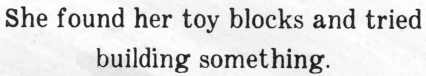

She found her toy blocks and tried
building something.

It worked!

Tilda started to feel
a bit better.

After that, she tried reading her favourite funny
book and laughed until her tummy ached.

Then she went out to play in the garden.

Everything still felt *very* strange.
But Tilda tried her best.

And the more Tilda *tried*,
the more she found
she COULD do.

Although there was one thing
that still felt too hard . . .

Tilda paused at the edge of the park
and watched her friends.
She almost left . . .

But then Tilda remembered the ladybird.

Could *she* be brave?
Could *she* keep trying?

Tilda decided that she *could*!

And it was the best decision
she ever made.

Even though her world
was still a little topsy turvy,
Tilda felt she could cope.

And because she felt she could cope,
her world seemed less
topsy turvy!

From that day on, whenever Tilda's world felt
a bit wobbly, she just tried her best.

And if that didn't work?

Tilda tried **again!**